For the Elders who have always shown us the way
— SFD & RD

To the matriarchs that speak to me most loudly when I'm standing alone on the shore
breathing in the fresh ocean air…Jenny St. Clair, Margarite Hamilton, Helen Rustanius Todd,
and my beautiful mom, Newborn Eagle Woman: Guud Jaada, Jackie Tyson
— JG

Canada Council   Conseil des arts
for the Arts   du Canada

We acknowledge the support of the Canada Council for the Arts.
Nous remercions le Conseil des arts du Canada de son soutien.

HighWater Press gratefully acknowledges the financial support of
the Province of Manitoba through the Department of Sport, Culture
and Heritage and the Manitoba Book Publishing Tax Credit, and the
Government of Canada through the Canada Book Fund (CBF),
for our publishing activities.

HighWater Press is an imprint of Portage & Main Press.
Printed and bound in Canada by Friesens
Design by Jennifer Lum
Cover Art by Janine Gibbons
Map by John Broadhead

Library and Archives Canada Cataloguing in Publication
Title: Jigging for halibut with Tsinii / by Sara Florence Davidson and
Robert Davidson ; illustrated by Janine Gibbons. Names: Davidson,
Sara Florence, 1973- author. | Davidson, Robert, 1946- author. |
Gibbons, Janine, illustrator.

Description: Series statement: Sk'ad'a ; 1 Identifiers: Canadiana (print)
20200399764 | Canadiana (ebook) 20200411071 | ISBN 9781553799818
(hardcover) | ISBN 9781553799825 (EPUB) | ISBN 9781553799832 (PDF)
Subjects: LCSH: Intergenerational relations—Juvenile literature. | LCSH:
Experiential learning—Juvenile literature. | LCSH: Indigenous peoples—
British Columbia—Haida Gwaii—Social life and customs—Juvenile
literature. | LCSH: Halibut fishing—Juvenile literature. | LCSH: Jigs (Fishing
lures)—Juvenile literature.

Classification: LCC HM726 .D38 2021 | DDC j306.4/2—dc23

25 24 23 22 21   1 2 3 4 5

HIGHWATER
PRESS
www.highwaterpress.com
Winnipeg, Manitoba
Treaty 1 Territory and homeland of the Métis Nation

JIGGING FOR HALIBUT with TSINII

SARA FLORENCE DAVIDSON | ROBERT DAVIDSON | JANINE GIBBONS

HIGHWATER
PRESS

My tsinii always knows when the weather is right for halibut jigging. He watches the ocean, and the sky, and the winds, and when it is right, he says, "We'll go out in the morning."

When morning comes, we push off the beach
in a dinghy that he built, and row into the inlet.
We always row with the tide.

Tsinii sits on a board across the gunnel and
rows forward in the way of the Elders. I sit
facing him on the bench and row backward,
my back toward the bow of the boat.

My hands grip the wooden oars that he made,
and we make our way down the inlet.

The wood knocks gently against the metal
locks in a steady rhythm.

We row for an hour
or so in silence.

My tsinii's eyes are old, and he cannot see as well as he used to, but he carefully watches the land. The rise of Tow Hill and the rocks of Wiia Point guide him to the halibut bank, better than my young eyes can.

Eventually, Tsinii stops rowing and says, "Okay, we'll fish here." He does not speak much English, so I know this means to put the anchor down.

I lift it up and heave it over the edge of the boat.

The anchor is swallowed by the ocean with a splash, and I am careful not to get caught in the rope as it quickly uncoils from the floor of the boat.

Once the anchor lands on the bottom of the ocean, we prepare the fishing lines, putting octopus on the halibut hooks for bait. Then we throw the lines out as far as we can and let them fall until they hit the bottom.

But they cannot rest there. If they remain on the ocean floor, the sea lice will get on the bait, and the halibut will not bite. So, I tug my line up a bit and begin the rhythmic movement with my arms, trying to lure the halibut to come to my bait.

The clouds are soft and blurred. It looks
like their jagged edges have been worn
away by the tides.

The waves gently lap against the sides
of the boat while the seagulls cry out,
chasing the feed in the ocean.

As I watch the clusters of groundswells
that have arrived here from afar, Tsinii says,
"It's going to blow northwest tomorrow."

Hours pass, and my arms begin to tire.
The halibut are not biting my bait today.

"HUP!" Tsinii's voice cries out.
He pulls hard on the line.
He has caught one!

I move quickly but carefully to his side with the
gaff in my hand. I am ready to club the halibut
so we can bring it onto the boat. Then Tsinii
starts to laugh, and I know I have been fooled.

The other end of his line is empty in the water.

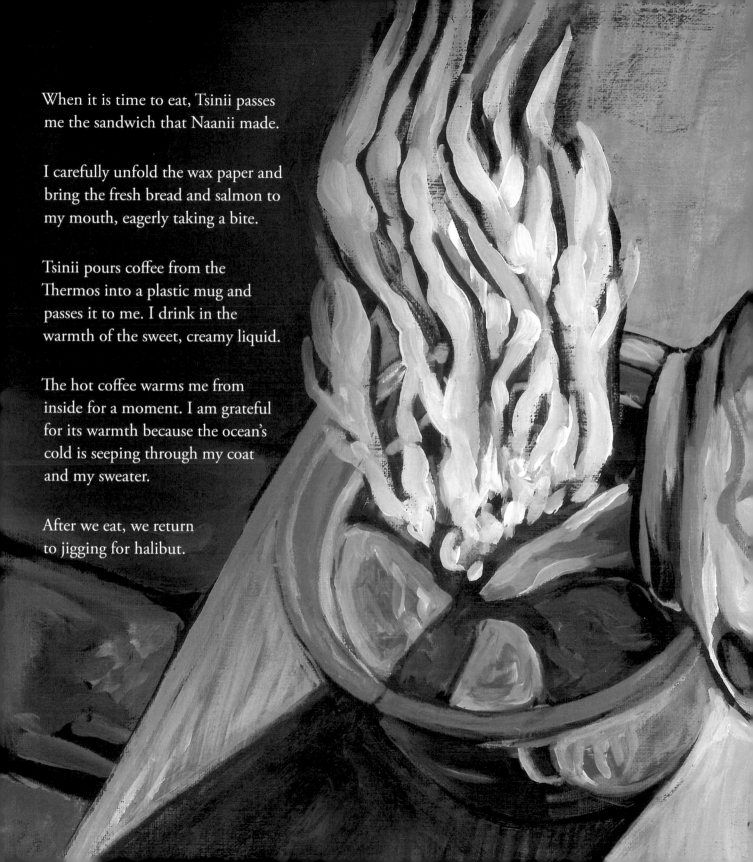

When it is time to eat, Tsinii passes
me the sandwich that Naanii made.

I carefully unfold the wax paper and
bring the fresh bread and salmon to
my mouth, eagerly taking a bite.

Tsinii pours coffee from the
Thermos into a plastic mug and
passes it to me. I drink in the
warmth of the sweet, creamy liquid.

The hot coffee warms me from
inside for a moment. I am grateful
for its warmth because the ocean's
cold is seeping through my coat
and my sweater.

After we eat, we return
to jigging for halibut.

"HUP!" Tsinii's voice cries out again, but this time I am
not so easily fooled. Instead of rushing over with the gaff,
I turn to smile at Tsinii.

But he is facing the water, tugging hard on his line.
I grab the gaff again and prepare to club the halibut when
it breaks through the surface of the water.

When it does, Tsinii says to the halibut, "Make your
mind strong because I'm going to club you."
This is out of respect, preparing the fish for
what is to come.

Tsinii brings the halibut into the boat, carefully placing it on the floor white belly side up. He takes out his new bait and puts it on the hook. "D'aal ts'ad Kaagaay," he murmurs quietly to the halibut as he rubs the bait onto the halibut's eyes. In Haida, he is telling the halibut to bite the bait and not just look at it. Then he throws the line out again.

I return to my bait and put it on my hook. Then I throw the line out into the ocean and jig some more.

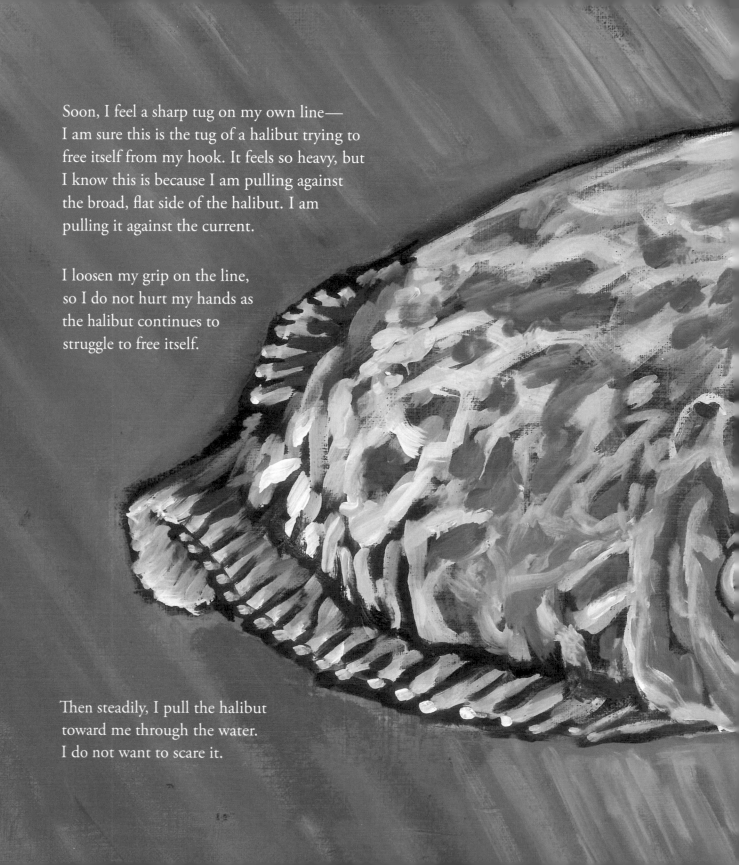

Soon, I feel a sharp tug on my own line—
I am sure this is the tug of a halibut trying to
free itself from my hook. It feels so heavy, but
I know this is because I am pulling against
the broad, flat side of the halibut. I am
pulling it against the current.

I loosen my grip on the line,
so I do not hurt my hands as
the halibut continues to
struggle to free itself.

Then steadily, I pull the halibut
toward me through the water.
I do not want to scare it.

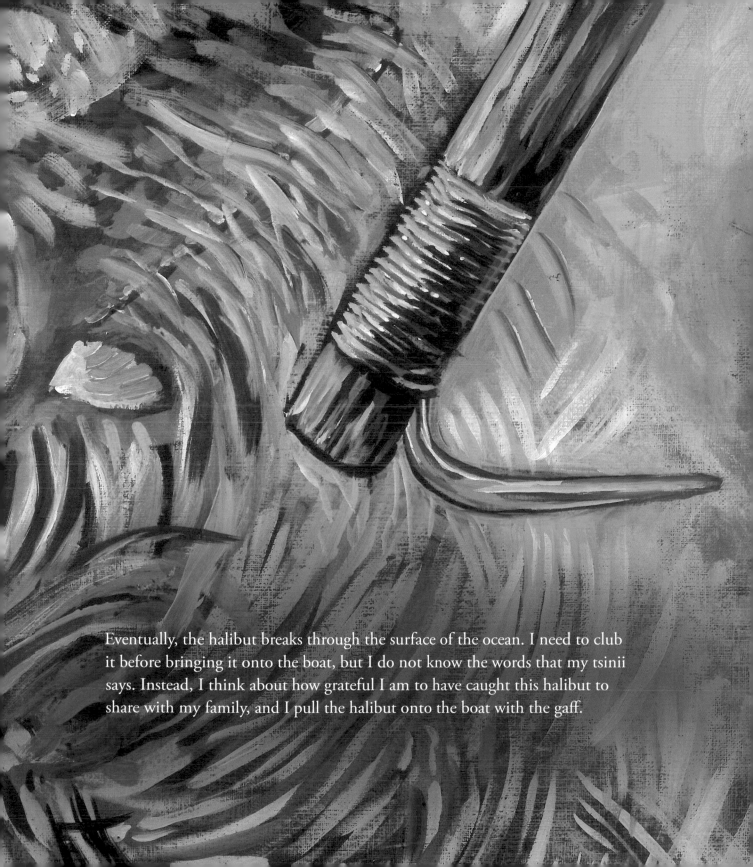

Eventually, the halibut breaks through the surface of the ocean. I need to club it before bringing it onto the boat, but I do not know the words that my tsinii says. Instead, I think about how grateful I am to have caught this halibut to share with my family, and I pull the halibut onto the boat with the gaff.

We do not catch any more halibut for the rest of the afternoon.
When the tide begins to shift, we know it is time to go home.
We must always travel with the tide.

I pull the anchor up and bring it back into the boat. Then I take the
oars in my hands again and begin pulling against the water.

My tsinii faces me and rows in the old way. We find that steady
rhythm once more as we row all the way back home.

When we arrive, I jump out of the boat and pull it up onto the beach, scraping it over the rocks and shells. I unload the halibut onto the beach as Tsinii climbs out of the boat. He pulls it up above the tide line and carefully ties it to a log.

On the beach, Tsinii and I clean the halibut together in silence.

There is no need to talk. He has already shown me how to clean the fish, so we work together to prepare the halibut for the family. As we clean the halibut, I think of my naanii in the kitchen preparing for our return, and I think of the halibut stew I know we will be eating for dinner tonight.

ABOUT THIS STORY

This story is based on real people and events. Sara and Robert talked about Robert's childhood memories of his tsinii. Sara used the information to create an imagined day of her father and his tsinii jigging for halibut.

ROBERT DAVIDSON SR.
gannyaa
1880–1969

The tsinii (grandfather) in this story is Robert Davidson Sr. He was a respected man of the Ts'aahl (Eagle) Clan in Old Massett. He was a skilled carpenter and helped build the local Anglican Church in 1919, designed and built his own houses, and was commissioned to build two traditional Haida canoes with his brother. He also built wooden seine boats including one called *Davidson Girl*. He was also a commercial fisherman, and he took up argillite carving in his later years. In 1969, he helped guide his grandson, Robert Davidson Jr. (author) on his pole raising in Old Massett. Robert Davidson Sr. was also was considered a keeper of the songs and shared much of this knowledge with Elders and community members in preparation for the pole raising. He was married to Florence Edenshaw Davidson, and they had 14 children together. Today, there are over 100 people from the village of Old Massett who are their direct descendants.

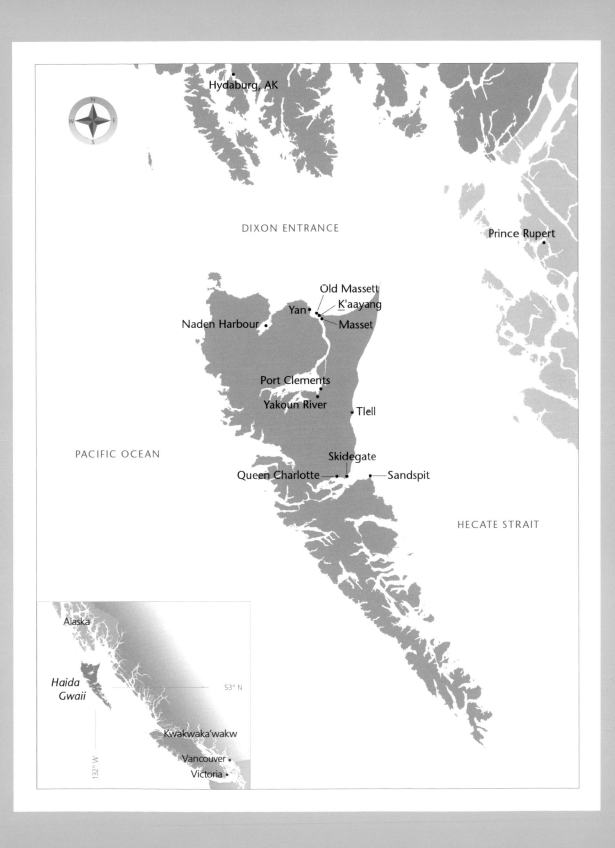

Hydaburg, AK

DIXON ENTRANCE

Prince Rupert

Old Massett
K̲'aayang
Yan
Naden Harbour
Masset

Port Clements
Yakoun River
Tlell

PACIFIC OCEAN

Skidegate
Queen Charlotte
Sandspit

HECATE STRAIT

Alaska

Haida Gwaii

53° N

Kwakwaka'wakw

132° W

Vancouver
Victoria